The Last
Dance

By: Britt Wolfe

Cover design, formatting, and caffeine consumption by Britt Wolfe. Additional emotional support provided by Sophie and Lena.

First Edition: 2025
ISBN: 978-1-0695065-8-0

Printed in Canada because books deserve a solid passport stamp too.

For inquiries, praise, declarations of undying love, or to request permission for use beyond fair dealing (seriously, just ask first), please visit: BrittWolfe.com

If you enjoyed this book, please consider leaving a review. If you didn't, well, that's between you and your questionable taste.

This Novella Is Dedicated to:

My own forever dance partner, my husband—a smoking hot Australian with a heart as steady as his laughter, as warm as the sun over the Pacific.

This story, though shaped by nostalgia and fleeting moments, was born from something timeless. Walter and Maggie's love was a season, a melody that played once and then faded into memory—but ours is a symphony, composed for a lifetime. I wanted to capture their magic, their momentary, incandescent love, in the way I feel about the life we have built together—a love that is breathtaking in its presence, in its certainty, in its forever.

For every dance, every laugh, every stolen glance that reminds me—we are the lucky ones.

The Last Dance
Is Inspired by: *Holy Ground (Taylor's Version)* by Taylor Swift

The Last Dance is inspired by *Holy Ground (Taylor's Version)* by Taylor Swift, a song that pulses with the rhythm of memory—love that was fleeting but bright, lost but never forgotten. This novella is not a story of forever, but of what once was and still lingers, of love that burned brilliantly in its time, even as the years folded it into something distant.

Walter and Maggie's story is one of youth, of dreams, of a love that felt like it could defy gravity. It is footsteps echoing in a grand old ballroom, the hum of a record spinning long after the music has ended, the weight of a name printed in black and white. It is the way some loves leave imprints that never fade, no matter how much time passes.

Because some places, some moments, some people—they are holy ground.

Peace, Love, and Inspiration,

Britt Wolfe

For Walter, his morning unfolded as it always did, with the quiet rustling of sheets and the slow, measured effort it took him to swing his legs over the side of the bed. His feet met the cool wooden floor, sending a brief shiver up his aging bones, but he welcomed it. It was a small reminder that he was still here, still tethered to the waking world. The house, a silent witness to his years of work and life, creaked softly as he moved—his own personal metronome, counting down the rhythm of his days.

He had lived alone for more years than he cared to count. There had been friends, once. A few. But time had a way of stripping life down to its barest bones. Now, it was just him, the house and his routine.

The kitchen greeted him with the comforting familiarity of its dim morning light, filtering through the lace curtains that had once belonged to his mother. The house sat on a quiet stretch of land outside of Houston, in a small, unincorporated community where the roads were lined with towering oaks and Spanish moss swayed lazily in the humid air. It was far enough from the city that the nights were still and silent, the stars unblemished by the artificial glow of downtown. In the mornings, the only sounds were the distant hum of crickets retreating into the brush and the occasional whistle of a train rolling through the countryside.

It had been his home for thirty years.

He reached for the coffee canister with the same practiced ease he had every morning. Black coffee. No sugar, no cream. The way his father drank it. The way he had learned to drink it in the early days of his career, when sleep was an inconvenience he couldn't afford. He had spent decades working for NASA, back when the Apollo program had consumed his every waking moment, when the world had its eyes turned toward the stars. Those long nights of calculations, of meticulous engineering, had been fueled by coffee just like this—strong, bitter, unwavering.

There had been a time when space exploration was everything to Walter, and to the world. When everyone held their breath as men walked on the moon, when people still believed that the stars were within reach. But the fervour had faded. The Apollo missions had given way to budget cuts, shifting priorities, and a collective disinterest from the public that once hung on every launch. Walter had poured himself into the work, sacrificing sleep, time, even love, to chase something bigger than himself. And now, when he looked at the night sky, he wondered if it had all been worth it. The world had moved on. The space race had become a relic, a chapter in history books. The things he had devoted his life to had been archived, reduced to museum exhibits and classroom discussions. And he —one of the countless people behind the curtain, the ones who had made it all happen—had been forgotten along with it.

He reached for the newspaper, the thin pages crackling beneath his fingertips as he unfolded them with care. The morning paper was a relic, much like him, much like his career. The world had turned to screens, to swipes and taps, to information delivered in fleeting headlines that disappeared as quickly as they appeared. He knew this well enough—his neighbours across the road, the Youngs, had a son, Jake, who had tried on more than one occasion to teach him how to use the touchscreen smartphone Walter had been forced to invest in. The boy had been patient, sitting beside Walter on the porch, explaining how he could read the news with just a few taps, how he could have everything at his fingertips in an instant.

But to Walter, there was no substitute for the morning paper. He liked the weight of it in his hands, the way the ink smudged his fingers, the slow, deliberate act of turning the pages. It was a part of his day he relished— one of the few things that remained unchanged in a world that seemed determined to leave him behind.

He took a sip of his coffee, turned a page. Another sip, another turn. He indulged in the unhurried pace of it. The slowness of his morning was one of the few luxuries that came with aging away from the man he had once been. There was a strange peace in watching the world from a distance, no longer tangled in the urgency of it all. This part of the morning—this ritual of ink-stained fingertips and quiet contemplation—was one of the good parts of growing old.

The names always came at the end. He never rushed to get there. He flipped through the world as it was—headlines about people who would be forgotten, stories about technology he no longer understood, articles that reminded him how far he had drifted from the centre of it all. And then, inevitably, the pages thinned, the ink grew smaller, and a procession of names waited for him.

It hadn't always been like this. There had been a time when he had skimmed past these pages, uninterested in the names of strangers, in the ceremonial rites of people he had never met. But everything had changed the year he retired. Only a few months after he left NASA, an old friend— Ed Koenig, one of the best engineers he had ever known—had passed away unexpectedly. The obituary had been buried in the back pages, a brief paragraph that barely scratched the surface of the man's brilliance. It had unsettled Walter in a way he hadn't anticipated. If Ed—sharp, strong, meticulous Ed—could go so suddenly, so quietly, then what did that mean for the rest of them? Since then, Walter had read the Births, Deaths And Marriages section religiously, as if tracking the names of the lost might prepare him for his own inevitable place among them.

Today, his gaze drifted down the page, the familiar rhythm of names and dates lulling him into complacency—until he saw it.

A woman's name.

His breath caught.

A name that brought memories and regret rushing to the surface, but also feelings of warmth and of perfect togetherness.

Margaret Wilkes.

Walter's fingers tightened around the paper, his pulse quickening. The name was printed in simple, unassuming typeface, tucked between strangers whose lives had never touched him. But hers—hers had been different.

Margaret Wilkes had been Margaret Dawson when he had known her.

Maggie.

She had been his once. Or perhaps he had been hers. It didn't matter now. The years had taken what they had and folded it into something distant, something unreachable. But seeing her name here—printed so plainly, so finally—made it feel as though she had just left him all over again.

His eyes skimmed the words, each one heavier than the last.

<u>Margaret Anne Wilkes (née Dawson)</u> Passed away peacefully in her sleep on the morning of March 2, 2025, at the age of 84. Margaret was the beloved wife of 62 years to Richard Wilkes and a devoted mother to four daughters: Elizabeth (Daniel) Carter, Julia (Mark) Reynolds, Katherine (Henry) Sullivan, and Abigail (James) Foster. She was a cherished grandmother to eight grandchildren: Eva, Benjamin, Anna, Nathan, Lucy, Evan, Amelia, and Aden. A gifted cellist, she performed with the Houston Symphony for over three decades, filling concert halls with warmth and grace. Beyond the stage, she dedicated herself to the performing arts, serving on the board of numerous charities and advocating for arts education. Even after retiring from the symphony, Margaret remained devoted to sharing the joy of music, offering free lessons to children in her community. She was a woman of kindness, conviction, and unwavering generosity. She will be deeply missed by her family, friends, and the many lives she touched. A memorial service will be held on March 6 at St. Andrews Church, followed by a private burial. In lieu of flowers, donations can be made to the Houston Youth Orchestra in her honour.

Walter read it again. And again. As if, by sheer will, he could force new words onto the page. Words that didn't describe the death a woman he had so loved, and who he so regretted losing.

But no obituary could capture what she had been. Not really. Not to him.

Margaret Dawson.

Maggie.

And then, as if time had peeled away like the delicate edge of a turning page, Walter was no longer an old man in his quiet kitchen. He was sixteen again, standing at the precipice of a different life, feeling as though he were growing into his body rather than shrinking out of it.

The air of the past had been thick with change that autumn, the kind that settled into the bones, lingering in the spaces between what had been and what was yet to come. The loss of his father had made everything sharper, heavier. It had been a folded flag and a somber ceremony, a Marine's final farewell, and then—nothing. Just silence. A quiet house with doors that didn't open the way they used to, a mother who moved through the days as if she were carrying a weight no one else could see. His older brother, James—strong, steady James—had done his best to fill the absence, but even he could only do so much.

And so, they had packed up what was left of their lives and left California behind. Houston had been waiting, sprawling and unfamiliar, with its broad streets and humid air, a city that seemed too alive for a family still steeped in grief. They moved into his maternal grandparents' home, a house filled with the scent of old books and lemon polish, with framed photographs that Walter's mother couldn't bring herself to look at too long. It was meant to be a place to steady themselves, to settle—but it had felt like standing at the edge of something vast and uncertain.

By the time he started school at Lamar High, winter was creeping in, though Texas cold bit sharper than California's ever had. The wind carried a chill that worked its way beneath collars and into bones, a different kind of cold than anything he'd known growing up near the Pacific. In Camp Pendleton, the winters had been mild, damp with the salt-laced breath of the ocean, the air soft even when the temperature dipped. But here, in Houston, the wind could be cruel, cutting through the streets with a dry, lingering bite, rattling the windows of his grandparents' home in the early hours of the morning. It wasn't snow and ice—not like the winters he'd read about in books—but it was enough to remind him that he was somewhere new. That everything was different now.

And then—her.

Across the corridor, just beyond the rows of lockers and passing voices, was a girl who seemed to brighten the very air around her. Her hair, golden and impossibly soft-looking, fell past her shoulders, catching the light in a way that made it seem almost illuminated. Her blue eyes, clear and endless, held an intensity that made people pause without knowing why, as though she saw the world in a way that no one else did. She moved with a quiet kind of confidence, effortless and sure, and when she laughed —soft but certain—it felt like something worth listening to.

Margaret Dawson.

For Walter, that simple, fleeting moment changed everything.

The cold was different here.

It wasn't the kind that cut straight to the bone, nor was it the damp chill of the Pacific air Walter had known all his life. Houston's winter settled heavy, pressing into the skin like an unwelcome hand, thick with moisture, clinging rather than biting. It made everything feel closer—the air, the walls, the weight of everything Walter and his family wasn't saying.

Walter shifted on the hard wooden chair in his grandparents' dining room, staring down at the untouched plate of eggs in front of him. The house was cramped, filled with the ghosts of the past—six children raised within these walls, though all had long since left, leaving behind their scuffed initials carved into doorframes and the echo of their voices trapped in the walls. The ceilings felt lower than they should have, the rooms smaller, and the air was thick with the scent of old books, mothballs, and bacon grease that never seemed to fade, no matter how many windows his grandmother cracked open.

It was somehow smaller than the housing on base in California had been. He hadn't thought that was possible.

James sat across from him, hunched over his plate, his fork scraping methodically against porcelain. Their mother sat next to him, silent, hands folded in her lap. She had been quiet ever since they'd arrived in Houston, her presence more of a shadow than a person.

Walter swallowed hard, gripping the edges of his chair. He wasn't sure if he could breathe in here.

Houston was supposed to be a fresh start. That's what everyone had said —his mother, his grandparents, the well-meaning neighbours who dropped off casseroles in those first few weeks after the funeral. A new city, a new home, a new beginning. But to Walter, it had never felt like anything more than an ending. Leaving California meant leaving behind everything familiar—his father's truck parked in the driveway, the distant crash of ocean waves, the warm scent of salt and sun lingering in the air. It meant leaving behind the base where his father had walked with purpose, where his uniform had still held meaning. Here, there were no echoes of him. His father had never set foot in this house, had never eaten at this table, had never walked these streets. His absence was absolute. And in the heavy quiet of the breakfast table, in the way his mother barely touched her food, Walter felt it pressing in from all sides. The move hadn't softened the loss—it had only made it sharper, more unbearable.

At school, it wasn't any better.

Lamar High was bigger than his last school—louder, faster. He had started a few months into his sophomore year, a stranger among kids who had known one another since they were small. The hallways smelled of chalk dust and floor wax, the air thick with the mingling scents of cheap cologne and the metallic bite of radiator heat. Everywhere he went, Walter felt like an intruder—like a book placed on the wrong shelf, slightly out of place, noticeable only when someone bothered to look closely.

He adjusted the strap of his bookbag and moved through the corridors, keeping his head down.

At his last school, he had known everyone. He had belonged. Now, everything was unfamiliar—voices he didn't recognize, teachers who called his name with uncertainty, unsure if he was worth remembering.

In the lunchroom, he took his tray to a table near the back, the noise a steady roar around him. Conversations swirled in the air, but none of them included him. He picked at his food, the taste of lukewarm mashed potatoes turning to paste in his mouth.

He missed home.

Not Houston. Not this new house, with its too-small rooms and walls that pressed too tightly around him.

Home.

The place where his father's presence still lingered.

Walter Callahan Sr.

The kind of man people looked up to. A Marine through and through— straight-backed, steady, unwavering. He had been strict, sure, but there had been comfort in his certainty. When he spoke, there was never any doubt. He had been the anchor of their family, the force that held them together, and now...

Now, there was only silence.

The funeral had been crisp and efficient, just as his father would have wanted. A folded flag, handed to his mother with solemn precision. A volley of shots fired into the air. The weight of uniforms and pressed shoulders, of men who had served alongside him standing in a stiff line, eyes forward, jaws set.

Walter had stood beside James, his hands clenched into fists at his sides, watching as his father was lowered into the ground. He had not cried.

Neither had James.

Their mother had, but even then, it had been quiet—just a few strangled sobs, her fingers gripping the edge of her coat.

Since then, she had faded into a ghost of herself, moving through the days as if she had forgotten how to live without Walter Sr.

And in some ways, maybe she had.

She was still there—physically. Still kissed her sons on the forehead in the mornings, still made sure they had what they needed. But her voice had lost its warmth, and she rarely met their eyes. It was like losing their father had hollowed her out, and now there was nothing left for them.

Walter didn't blame her for it.

But his heart was broken by it.

*****

The morning Walter met Maggie, breakfast was a quiet affair.

Walter sat at the kitchen table, the scent of bacon and coffee hanging heavy in the warm, too-small room. His grandmother had cooked, as she always did, and his grandfather sat at the head of the table, occasionally muttering about something he read in the paper. James ate steadily, moving with a certainty Walter envied. Their mother, however, barely touched her food.

The quiet of the morning wasn't peaceful. It wasn't restful. It was the kind of silence that pressed in on the lungs, making it difficult to breathe.

James spoke first. "I put in an application for an early enlistment program."

Their mother's fingers tensed around her coffee cup, but she said nothing. She didn't look up.

James continued, voice measured. "It won't start until after I graduate, but at least I'll have a plan."

Walter stared at his plate, his appetite gone.

James wanted this. He always had. Stepping into their father's shoes wasn't just a choice for him—it was a calling, as natural as breathing. Walter, on the other hand, could no longer see past tomorrow, let alone picture a future for himself. The loss, the move, the so-called fresh start that everyone insisted on, but that felt more like the abrupt ending to a life he had barely begun—all of it pressed against his chest, heavy and painful, like something physical and sharp inside of himself. It threatened to spill over, to crack through the fragile control he clung to. And so, he took it day by day, hour by hour, holding it all inside because that was the only way he knew how to keep moving.

Their mother said nothing.

She simply rose from the table, movements careful, deliberate, as if anything too sudden might shatter the fragile balance of the morning. She didn't look at them, didn't speak. Just pushed back her chair with a whisper-soft scrape of wood against tile and walked out of the kitchen, her hands trembling slightly as they smoothed over the front of her sweater.

Walter watched as she disappeared down the hall, the door to her childhood bedroom closing behind her with a quiet finality.

For a long moment, no one spoke.

The silence settled like dust, filling the spaces between them, thick and suffocating. The clatter of a fork against porcelain, the low murmur of the radio humming from the counter near the stove—these were the only sounds that dared to break the stillness.

Their grandmother cleared her throat softly, her voice an offering. "Your mother is probably just worried about you," she said, though her words were meant for James. "You're still so young."

She reached for the serving spoon, the movement familiar, automatic. More scrambled eggs landed on James's plate, though he hadn't asked for them.

James barely glanced up. "Dad was young when he enlisted."

The words were quiet. Even. But they struck like a stone dropped into deep water, sending ripples through the room.

Their grandmother flinched.

The conversation ended.

Walter pushed his eggs around his plate, his appetite long gone.

The warmth from the stove still lingered in the air, mixing with the scent of coffee and grease, but it did nothing to thaw the cold inside his chest.

A few minutes later, he and James stepped outside, the morning air biting sharp against their skin.

The door clicked shut behind them.

Walter pulled his coat tighter around himself, but the cold had already settled deep, and he knew—no matter how many layers he wore—it wasn't going anywhere. Houston's winter wasn't the bitter kind, but it clung to his skin in a way that California's never had. He walked beside James in silence, listening to the gravel crunch beneath their feet.

James shoved his hands into his coat pockets. "You've gotta think about what you want to do after school."

Walter let out a slow breath, watching it cloud in the cold.

James glanced at him. "Come on, you must have some idea."

Walter shook his head.

His brother sighed. "You don't have to decide today. But just... think about it."

Walter didn't respond.

The school loomed ahead.

As they neared the entrance, James spotted a group of seniors near the steps. He gave Walter a quick nod before peeling away, sliding seamlessly into the fold of conversation, laughter, and easy camaraderie.

Walter hesitated.

James had found his place.

Walter wasn't sure he ever would.

He turned, letting his shoulders sag slightly, moving through the halls like a prisoner.

The day stretched ahead, heavy, endless. He couldn't see past it.

And then—

He saw her.

Impossible.

She was walking toward him.

The noise of the hallway—the laughter, the clatter of books, the distant voice of a teacher calling for students to hurry—faded into something muted, background static.

She moved with an effortless kind of grace. Not the sort that demanded attention, but the kind that made people pause without realizing why. Her golden hair cascaded over her shoulders, catching the dim glow of the overhead lights, turning it almost silver at the edges. Her blue eyes were bright, searching.

And then, impossibly, they landed on him.

Walter's breath stilled.

"Walter Callahan, right?"

Her voice was soft but assured. Rich and deep.

He couldn't speak.

She smiled—not a big smile, just the smallest tilt of her lips, as if she understood his silence.

"I'm Margaret. Well, people call me Maggie," she extended her hand with a smile and Walter shook it meekly. "I always see you by yourself," she said, her words making colour rise in his cheeks.

His heart pounded.

She tilted her head slightly. "Would you like to eat lunch with me today?"

Walter stared.

She gave a small laugh. "I'm a freshman, so we don't have any of the same classes. But I figured... maybe you'd like the company."

He could only nod.

Her smile widened, and then, just like that, she turned—her movement light, elegant, effortless as a deer. She disappeared into the sea of students, leaving behind nothing but the lingering echo of her presence.

Walter let out a breath.

The morning stretched before him, but for once, it wasn't just something to endure—it was something to get through, a series of meaningless hours standing between him and seeing Maggie again.

He barely made it through his classes.

Every moment crawled, each lesson seeming long and longer, beyond reason. His teachers spoke, but their words were lost to the static in his head. He scribbled half-formed notes, but his mind wasn't on the equations or historical dates.

Lunch.

He just had to make it to lunch.

By the time the bell rang, his pulse was hammering.

He grabbed his tray, scanning the cafeteria, nerves pulling at the edges of his stomach.

And then, there she was. Maggie.

Sitting by a window, the soft afternoon light draping over her shoulders. She caught sight of him, lifting her hand slightly in greeting.

Somehow, he managed to move his feet.

He slid into the seat across from her, gripping his tray like it was the only thing tethering him to the ground.

She smiled. "You made it."

He nodded.

She unwrapped her sandwich. "I usually eat outside, but it's too cold now."

Walter still hadn't spoken.

She didn't seem to mind. She took a bite, then gestured at his tray. "Are you going to eat?"

Walter blinked down at the unappetizing pile of mashed potatoes and green beans. He hesitated, then picked up his fork.

She grinned. "That's a good start."

They ate in companionable silence for a while. He wasn't sure how it happened, but somehow, his shoulders eased. Somehow, it didn't feel so strange to be sitting across from her.

Maggie told him about Austin. About how she had only moved to Houston the summer before.

"I know what it's like to be new," she said. "To feel like you don't belong."

Walter glanced at her.

She hesitated, then added, "I heard about your dad."

His grip tightened on his fork.

"We live a few doors down from your grandparents. My older sister, Beverly, watered their plants when they went to California to help you pack," she explained. "I just... I wanted to say I'm sorry." Her voice was gentle. "But that's not why I asked you to sit with me."

Walter looked at her fully.

She held his gaze. "I just thought... maybe you could use a friend."

His throat tightened. Maggie couldn't possibly understand just how true her words were.

For months, Walter had felt hollow—like something essential had been carved out of him the day his father died, leaving only a vast, aching emptiness behind. Grief had settled inside him like a slow-moving tide, rising and falling but never retreating. And now, in this unfamiliar city, surrounded by people who were supposed to feel like family but still felt like strangers, that emptiness only deepened.

His grandparents were kind, but their house wasn't home. His mother was here, but not really—what was left of her was quiet and faded, like a photograph left too long in the sun. And James...James had adapted. James had found his place. James had always known where he was headed.

Walter, meanwhile, felt unglued.

Floating.

Alone in everything.

Before he could find words to express himself, Maggie smiled again. "Do you want to walk home together after school?"

He nodded.

And for the first time in a long time, the day didn't feel so heavy.

With school letting out for the day, the afternoon sun had begun its slow descent by the time Walter and Maggie left the school grounds, the air still thick with the remnants of the day's warmth. The sky, a pale and endless stretch above them, was smeared with the first traces of dusk—lavender and peach, fading into the deepening blue of evening.

They walked side by side, their steps in quiet rhythm against the pavement. Walter, ordinarily so cautious with his words, found himself speaking more easily than he had in months. Maggie, he was finding, had that effect him—it wasn't that she demanded conversation, but rather that she created a space where silence felt like an invitation, rather than a void.

"So, what's your story, Walter Callahan?" Maggie asked, her voice light, like they weren't still half-strangers walking home together.

Walter hesitated. He wasn't used to people asking about him—not in a way that made him feel like the answer mattered. But Maggie had a way of making things feel effortless, like she wasn't just filling the space between them but actually wanted to hear what he had to say.

"Not much of one," he admitted. "Just trying to get used to a new place."

She adjusted the strap of her bookbag. "It takes time. Houston's big, and folks don't always take to newcomers right away."

Walter glanced at her. "You ever lived anywhere else?"

She shook her head. "Nope. Born and raised. My daddy grew up in our house, same as me. Says he remembers your uncle from when they were kids."

Walter nodded. That made sense. His mother had grown up here, but somehow, it still didn't feel like his family belonged—or maybe it was just that he didn't feel like he had much of a family left. But then, out of the corner of his eye, he caught Maggie's gentle smile, and just like that, the thought slipped away, quiet and fleeting, like a wave retreating from the shore.

For a few moments, they walked in comfortable silence.

Maggie glanced at him again. "Your brother settling in alright?"

Walter shrugged. "James can fit in anywhere." It was one of the many attributes Walter had always admired about her older brother.

She nodded, as if that answer didn't surprise her. "I heard he's planning to enlist."

Walter glanced at her, surprised. "You heard that?" Walter was still learning just how small Houston actually was.

She smiled slightly. "Word gets around. And besides, your grandparents and my parents are really friendly."

Walter exhaled, shaking his head. "Yeah. James has it all figured out."

Maggie considered that for a moment. "And you?"

Walter hesitated.

He thought about California—the crash of the waves, the smell of salt in the air, the way the world had seemed bigger there. His father had belonged to that world. James had a plan. But Walter?

"I don't know yet," he admitted.

Maggie smiled, slow and knowing. "Well," she said, "you've got time."

She glanced at him, a small smile tugging at the corner of her lips. "I like how quiet you are."

Walter blinked. "Yeah?" He hadn't thought of himself as quiet—at least, not before.

She nodded. "Some boys talk just to hear themselves. You don't. I can tell when you're thinking about things."

He didn't know what to say to that, so he just kept walking, but something about her words sat warm in his chest.

They turned down a quiet street, the houses familiar but still foreign to Walter. He had walked this route every day since he'd arrived in Houston, but it had never felt like his neighbourhood. But with Maggie beside him, it didn't feel quite so unfamiliar.

After a few more steps, she slowed. "This is me," she said, nodding toward a house with a wide front porch. The light was on inside, casting a welcoming glow against the lowering light of the late afternoon.

Walter stopped beside her, suddenly feeling awkward, like he'd reached the end of something he didn't want to be over just yet.

Maggie hesitated, shifting on her feet. Then, before she could talk herself out of it, she said, "There's a winter dance coming up."

Walter blinked. "Oh?"

She smiled, a little nervous but still certain. Her blue eyes caught the light as she looked at Walter. "I was wondering if you'd go with me."

He stared at her, momentarily stunned.

"I know boys are supposed to ask," she added quickly. "But you're new, and I figured... I mean, if you want to."

He found his voice just in time. "I—yeah. Yeah, I'd like that."

Her smile widened, and something warm settled in Walter's chest, something unfamiliar, but undeniably good.

"Okay," she said softly.

Neither of them moved for a second, standing there in the fading sunlight. Then, just as she turned to go, Maggie hesitated, glanced at him, and— tentatively, hesitantly—reached for his hand.

Walter stopped breathing. He wondered if girls knew the power they had —to steal the air from a boy's lungs with just a look, to turn his whole world upside down with the touch of a hand.

Her fingers were warm against his, small and certain. She gave his hand the smallest squeeze, watching him carefully. He looked down at their joined hands, then back up at her, a slow smile spreading across his face.

Maggie grinned, then let go, stepping back toward the porch. "I'll see you tomorrow. Walk me to school?" Her voice was light, hopeful.

He nodded, still dazed. "Yeah. Tomorrow."

She turned, opening the front door, then hesitated just before stepping inside. She looked back at him one more time, her smile lingering, then disappeared into the house.

Walter exhaled a breath he hadn't realized he was holding.

Then, with his heart still racing, he walked the short distance to his grandparents' house, a smile tugging at the corner of his lips. The first real smile he'd felt since the day his father's training exercise at Camp Pendleton went terribly wrong—since the misfire that took his life in an instant, sudden and unforgiving.

As Walter climbed the three steps up to his grandparents' porch, his heart was light, with a warmth settling in his chest. He had no way of knowing it yet, but that afternoon had changed everything.

Because Maggie Dawson would be the love of his life.

It Was Good
1957

The night air was thick with the lingering warmth of the Houston summer, the heat of the day still trapped in the pavement, radiating upward in slow waves. The world had softened into twilight, the last embers of sunlight sinking below the horizon, leaving behind a sky streaked with deep purples and soft oranges. Fireflies flickered lazily in the humid air, their tiny sparks winking in and out of existence like fleeting memories.

Walter's 1950 Chevrolet Styleline Deluxe sat parked beneath the towering oaks near Buffalo Bayou, where the city lights shimmered in the distance, reflected in the dark, still water. It wasn't much—not compared to the fancy cars some of his classmates had been gifted for graduation—but it was his. He had worked for it, pouring his after-school hours at the hardware store into every scratched-up dollar that had gone toward buying it. The paint was a little worn, the radio crackled now and then, but it ran. And it had a bench seat wide enough that Maggie could sit close, her bare knee brushing against his in the dim light.

Walter's graduation had unfolded like a dream, slipping past him in quiet, golden moments he could hardly hold onto. His grandparents had been there, their faces alight with a pride that settled deep in his chest, warm and steady. And Maggie—Maggie, who had walked into his life on a quiet afternoon two years ago and never left. Maggie, who had become woven into the very fabric of him, as natural as breath, as certain as the setting sun.

But his mother hadn't come.

She couldn't.

And James—James was at Camp Lejeune, locked into the rigid demands of training, where leave was a privilege rarely granted to junior enlisted men. A letter had arrived two days before, short and stiff, its words careful but distant. He was proud of Walter, wished he could be there, but the Corps came first, and there was no bending the rules—not for a graduation, not for anything short of emergency orders. Walter hadn't expected him to make it, but still, the absence sat heavy in his chest, an ache he couldn't shake.

Maggie didn't have to ask what was up. She already knew.

She reached for his hand, her fingers warm, certain—the kind of touch that anchored, that told him without words that she was there. "You're thinking about them."

Walter swallowed, his gaze fixed on the windshield, where the city lights stretched endlessly ahead, blurred by the weight in his chest. "Yeah."

She didn't rush to fill the silence, didn't try to pull him away from it. That was the thing about Maggie—she never asked him to be anything other than what he was. She just laced her fingers through his, holding on, like she always had. Like she always would.

"I know you wanted them there," she said after a while, her voice quiet, thoughtful.

Walter let out a breath. "James couldn't get leave."

Maggie nodded. "And your mom?"

He hesitated, his fingers flexing against the steering wheel. "She's still at

Saint Mary's."

It was the first time he had said it out loud—to anyone.

Saint Mary's Home for the Infirmed, one of the many institutions scattered across Texas, meant for people like her—people who had disappeared into themselves and couldn't come back.

She had lasted as long as she could. But after a year in Houston, after James left for the Marines and Walter was left with the silence, it had become clear—she wasn't going to get better.

She had slipped further away, her mind folding in on itself, trapping her inside a world Walter couldn't reach. She had stopped getting out of bed. Stopped eating unless prompted. Stopped responding at all.

And so, one day, his grandparents had taken her to Saint Mary's.

Walter had gone to see her, at first. He had sat beside her, telling her about school, about James, about Maggie. She had stared past him, through him, lost in some place he couldn't follow. Eventually, his grandmother had told him to stop going—that it was too much for him, that it wouldn't help. And after a while, he had listened.

Maggie squeezed his hand, bringing him back to the present.

"I'm sorry," she said, and he knew she meant it.

Walter could always feel Maggie—in the quiet, in the certainty of her presence. And in that moment, he felt her in his disappointment too, like she was carrying the weight of it with him.

Walter let out a slow breath. "Yeah. Me too."

They sat in silence for a long moment, the air between them thick, heavy—dense with everything unsaid, everything felt but not spoken. The weight of it settled in Walter's chest, pressing against his ribs, a quiet ache that had no name, only presence. The night stretched wide around them, the hum of cicadas filling the spaces where words should have been, but still, the silence held.

Then Maggie leaned into him, resting her head against his shoulder, and the weight in his chest softened, unraveling like a knot coming undone. Her warmth bled into him, steady and certain, and in that moment, it was as if she had reached inside him and gathered up every aching piece, holding them together with nothing more than her presence.

She was warm against him, familiar in the way that only Maggie could be. She smelled like vanilla and something softer, something sweeter, something that had always belonged to her alone. The night seemed to be enveloping them—the slow croak of frogs from the bayou, the quiet lap of water against the bank, the occasional crackle of the cooling engine beneath the hood.

Walter exhaled, tipping his head slightly toward hers.

"I love you," Maggie murmured, her voice so soft it nearly disappeared into the dark.

Walter closed his eyes for a moment, letting it settle into him, the way it always did. He had lost count of how many times she had said it, and how many times he had said it back, but somehow, it still stirred something in him every time.

"I know," he said, pressing a slow, warm kiss into her hair.

A small, knowing smile played at her lips. "You could say it back."

He turned toward her then, watching the way the faint glow of the city lights flickered in her blue eyes, making them look almost unreal. He had known her face for years—knew every expression, every flicker of thought before she spoke it aloud—but she still had a way of making him breathless.

"I love you, Maggie Dawson," he murmured.

She smiled, but there was something else in it tonight. Something slower, something weighted.

Walter felt it before she moved, the shift in the air between them, the way her fingers trailed lightly along his forearm before she turned toward him fully, her knees brushing against his.

Then she kissed him, and he felt it everywhere.

It was different tonight. Not urgent, not rushed, but deliberate. A slow unraveling, a knowing. Her lips were soft, warm, insistent in a way that made the world outside the car fall away, lost to the stillness of the bayou and the quiet hum of her breath against his skin.

Walter reached for her, his fingers finding her waist, pulling her closer as he deepened their kiss. Maggie let him, pressing against him like she had been waiting for this—like they had both been waiting for this without knowing it.

Her hands slid up his chest, slow and searching, the tips of her fingers tracing the collar of his shirt before tangling into his chestnut hair. Walter's breath hitched.

There had been kisses before. Countless stolen moments in darkened hallways, in the front seat of this car, in the soft quiet of her bedroom when no one was home. But this was different. This was the edge of something unknown, something inevitable.

Maggie's lips parted slightly against his, her breath warm, her touch electric.

Walter moved carefully, deliberately, like this moment was something sacred, something holy—because to him, it was. He met it with reverence, with the quiet awe of someone who understood he was stepping into something that would never leave him. His hands traced the curve of her back, slow and certain, pulling her into him, and she followed without hesitation, her body pressing against his as if she had always belonged there.

The car was too small for the way they needed each other, but neither of them cared. The leather seat creaked as Maggie shifted, settling into his lap, her arms wrapped around his neck. Walter let out a slow, shuddering breath, his hands skimming her thighs, feeling the way her breath caught at the contact.

She was everywhere—her scent, her warmth, the way she moved against him with knowing tenderness, as if she had always been meant to be here, in this moment, with him.

Maggie pulled back just slightly, just enough to look at him, her lips red, kiss-swollen. "Are you sure?" she whispered.

Walter's hands slid higher, fingers trailing over the soft fabric of her dress, feeling the way her breath quickened beneath his touch.

His answer was a kiss—deep, slow, devotional—like something sacred. "If you are," he murmured, his lips brushing against hers, their breath mingling in the hush of the night.

Maggie sighed into him, sinking deeper, her fingers gripping his shoulders as if holding onto something unshakable, something sacred. There was no hesitation, no uncertainty—only the quiet surrender of two souls meeting in the space where longing became something holier.

Outside, the world moved on—the fireflies still blinking, the water still lapping, the night stretching long and endless around them. But here, in the hush between heartbeats, time knelt at their feet and waited.

And when it moved again, when breath met breath and touch became something eternal, nothing was the same.

In the quiet that followed, Walter held Maggie against him, his hand trailing slow, absentminded circles against the bare skin of her back. Her forehead was damp, a soft sheen catching in the dim light, and her blue eyes fluttered open, heavy-lidded, searching for his gaze. She looked like something celestial, something made of stardust and softness, and for the first time in his life, he understood what all the songs were about—the ones draped in veiled metaphors and whispered longing, the ones that spoke of love like a force of nature, uncontainable, inevitable.

Maggie sighed, nestling closer, her fingertips grazing along his collarbone.

"What are you thinking about?"

Walter let out a breath of a laugh. "Songs."

She tilted her head up at him, amusement flickering in her drowsy smile. "Songs?"

He nodded, brushing a strand of golden hair from her cheek. "All those songs about love... about fire, and fever, and never wanting the night to end. I used to think they were just words." He kissed her forehead, lingering there for a moment, feeling the way her breath slowed against his skin. "Now, I get it."

Maggie's smile softened. "Yeah?"

He pulled back just enough to see her fully, to take in the way she was watching him, like she already knew what he was going to say before he even said it. His heart knocked against his ribs, not with nerves but with certainty.

"I've been thinking about next year," he murmured.

Maggie's fingers stilled against his skin. "And?"

Walter exhaled slowly, staring past the windshield, where the night stretched wide and endless before them. "I don't know what I want to do yet... not really," he admitted. "But I know that studying mechanical engineering will open doors for me. I got into Rice." He let the words settle between them, still half-disbelieving them himself. "It's a good school. A damn good school. And maybe if I go there, I'll find my way to something I actually want. Or at least something I am good at." He swallowed, his fingers absently tracing patterns along Maggie's skin. "But what I do know —what I don't have a single doubt about—is that I need to be here. With you."

His gaze flickered to hers, searching for understanding, for something that told him she knew what he was trying to say. "I don't have some grand plan, Maggie," he murmured. "I just know that I want to figure it out with you."

She looked at him for a long moment, her expression unreadable, until finally, she whispered, "You mean that?"

"With everything I am." He took her hand, tracing the delicate lines of her fingers with his thumb. Slowly, he brought it to his lips, pressing a kiss to the pad of her thumb, then each fingertip in turn, lingering just long enough to make her breath hitch. When he reached her third finger—the one reserved for promises, for forevers, the one people put wedding rings on—he hesitated for a moment, then kissed it softly, reverently, as if sealing something unspoken between them.

Maggie let out a breath, shaky and light, like something inside her had just loosened. She smiled a smile so radiant it stole the air from his lungs, and Walter knew—this was it. This was the moment.

Carefully, he reached over to the glove compartment and pulled out the small velvet box he had been keeping there for days, waiting for the right time. His hands were steady, though his heart pounded as he flipped it open, revealing the delicate gold band inside.

Maggie's lips parted, her breath catching.

"It's not an engagement ring," he said quickly, searching her face. "I know we're young. I know we've got time. You haven't even finished high school yet. But I also know that there won't be anyone else, not for me. So I—I wanted to give you something. Something to promise that no matter where life takes us, no matter how long it takes me to figure things out, you'll be the one I come home to."

Maggie didn't say anything at first. She just looked at him, at the promise ring, then back at him, like she was memorizing this moment, pressing it into the deepest part of herself. Then, slowly, she lifted a trembling hand and let him slide the ring onto her finger. It was a perfect fit.

Maggie blinked, her lashes damp, and when she finally spoke, her voice was barely above a whisper. "Walter Callahan, I love you so much it scares me."

Walter cupped her face, brushing his thumb over her cheek, his voice just as quiet. "I know the feeling."

And then she kissed him, slow and deep, and the night wrapped around them, holding them in a world all their own.

Where We Stood
1959

The winter air in Houston still carried a crispness, but one that rarely lingered, a fleeting bite that softened before it could truly settle. After four years in the city, Walter was used it. The streets outside the restaurant glowed under the golden haze of streetlamps, reflecting in the rain-damp pavement, giving the city a quiet, dreamlike shimmer.

Walter guided Maggie through the entrance of Tony's, an elegant little restaurant tucked in the heart of the city, the kind of place that felt special, meant for occasions that mattered. He had saved for weeks to bring her here, wanting the night to be perfect. As the host led them to their table, Walter pulled out her chair before she could reach for it herself.

Maggie smiled up at him as she took her seat, her blue eyes full of softness. "A gentleman," she teased, settling the folds of her dress before resting her hands on the table.

Walter smirked as he took his seat across from her. "Only for you."

For a moment, they simply looked at one another, the quiet hum of the restaurant wrapping around them—the gentle clinking of glasses, the low murmur of conversations, the scent of butter and wine in the air. Then, at the exact same time, they both opened their mouths.

"I have something to tell you," Walter said, just as Maggie blurted, "I have news."

They stopped, eyes widening before breaking into laughter, their voices overlapping again as they both gestured for the other to go first.

"No, you first," Walter said, grinning.

Maggie shook her head. "No way, you first."

They laughed again, caught in the easy rhythm of four years of knowing each other better than anyone else.

Maggie reached for her water glass, arching a brow. "Alright, Callahan. What's this big news of yours?"

Walter took a breath, the weight of what he was about to say settling in. He hadn't planned on telling her like this, but now, sitting across from her in the soft glow of the restaurant, there was no one else in the world he wanted to share his news with.

"I got a letter from a recruiter." He leaned forward slightly, his voice steady, measured. "From NASA."

Maggie stilled, her glass hovering just inches from her lips. "NASA?"

He nodded. "It's new, barely a year old, but they're already working on getting Americans into space. They're recruiting engineers—people who know how to design, build, test things for flight. I guess someone at Rice put my name forward."

Maggie set her glass down carefully. "Walter." She exhaled his name, her eyes bright with something between awe and disbelief. "That's incredible."

Walter rubbed the back of his neck, still processing it himself. "Yeah, it is. I mean, it's not an offer yet. They're looking at people, seeing who might be a good fit, but..." He paused, searching for the right words. "For the first time, I feel like I know what I want to do."

Maggie's expression softened, her hands folding over his on the table. "Tell me."

Walter's chest tightened—not with fear, but with certainty. "I think I want to be part of it. I want to build something that goes up there." He glanced toward the ceiling as if space itself were just beyond it. "Can you imagine? The first American in orbit? And I'd get to be one of the people making that happen."

Maggie's lips parted, her fingers tightening around his. "Walter, that's—" She shook her head slightly, a slow smile spreading across her face. "That's amazing."

His grin grew. "Yeah?"

"Yeah," she said softly. "You finally have your answer."

Walter exhaled, letting himself sink into the truth of that. "I think I do."

She squeezed his hand once more before leaning back, her own excitement rising again. "Alright, well, if you think your news is going to outshine mine, you're sorely mistaken."

Walter chuckled. "Oh? Let's hear it."

Maggie straightened, her chin lifting slightly, eyes gleaming. "I was offered a spot in the Houston Youth Symphony."

Walter blinked. "Maggie—"

"I start next season," she continued, voice bubbling over with pride and joy. "It's one of the best pre-professional symphonies in the country, and if I do well there... it's a direct pathway to the Houston Symphony. My dream job. My dream orchestra. Walter, I might be a cellist in the Houston Symphony!"

Walter couldn't stop the grin from spreading across his face. "Maggie, that's..." He shook his head. "That's incredible."

She beamed, her hands fluttering slightly, excitement making her unable to sit still. "It's more than I ever expected for my first year at the conservatory. I was going to audition next year, but one of my professors recommended me early."

Walter could see it in her—the way she practically vibrated with happiness, the way she came alive when she talked about music. It was her calling, the way engineering was starting to feel like his.

"What does it mean?" he asked. "Like, for your studies, for you?"

She bit her lip, thinking. "It means rehearsals every week, performances at major venues, working with conductors who could get me into bigger programs later on. It means everything."

Walter sat back, shaking his head in amazement. "Maggie Dawson, future cellist of the Houston Symphony."

She laughed, reaching for her water glass. "I'll drink to that."

Walter lifted his glass. "To the Houston Symphony. And to NASA."

Their glasses clinked together, the sound crisp, full of promise.

They had met as teenagers, tangled in grief, in uncertainty, in the unknown of their own futures. And now, here they were—on the edge of something great.

Something that, for the first time, they could see clearly.

Something that belonged to them.

Later, outside the restaurant, the winter air wrapped around them, crisp and edged with the scent of damp pavement and the distant sweetness of orange blossoms. The city hummed quietly around them—car engines murmuring, distant laughter spilling from open doorways, the occasional echo of a passing streetcar rattling in the distance. But in this moment, it was only them.

Maggie's gloved hand curled around Walter's, her fingers threading easily through his like they had always belonged there. She tipped her head back, her golden hair catching the glow of the streetlights, and for a moment, she just watched him—like she was memorizing him, storing away this moment, this exact feeling.

Walter swallowed against the emotion swelling in his throat. He had always thought of the future in shadows, a blurry shape he could never quite define. But tonight, with Maggie beside him, laughing softly into the cold, her eyes alight with something so full of promise, the future didn't feel so unknowable.

It felt like her.

It felt like this.

A rare flurry of snow began to drift from the sky, a whisper of white against the deep Houston night. It was the kind of moment that didn't belong here, a fleeting kind of magic that came once in a lifetime—like this night, like them. The flakes caught in Maggie's hair, delicate as lace, melting almost as soon as they landed. She reached up, brushing a few from his collar, her fingers lingering just a moment longer than necessary, signalling that she, too, understood that this night—this snowfall, this feeling—was something they would never forget.

Walter exhaled a breath that curled in the cold. "Four years," he murmured, shaking his head slightly, as if the passage of time itself surprised him.

Maggie smiled, her fingers still ghosting over the lapel of his coat. "And forever to go."

She said it like it was certain, like it was written in the stars. And for the first time, Walter let himself believe it.

He lifted her hand to his lips, pressing a kiss to her gloved knuckles, sealing the moment between them.

Somewhere in the distance, the clock in the town square chimed the hour, a deep, reverberating sound that carried through the quiet night.

And just like that, the rest of their lives stretched out before them.

Footprints On The Sidewalk

1961

Maggie sat on a wrought-iron bench in Sam Houston Park, her cello case resting against her leg, the weight of it settling her as the late afternoon light stretched long across the brick pathways. The air was crisp for a Houston fall, carrying the scent of damp earth and the distant sweetness of magnolia trees. Wind stirred the branches above her, rustling the stubborn golden leaves that clung to their branches, unwilling to accept the turn of the season.

Walter was late. Thirty minutes late.

She pulled her coat tighter around herself, pressing her lips together as she glanced toward the path leading from the street. Nothing. No hurried steps, no familiar figure weaving through the trees, his tie loosened from the day, his hair tousled from running his hands through it.

She exhaled slowly, forcing herself to be patient.

It wasn't the first time he had been late. Lately, it felt like he was always running behind, always caught up at work, always distracted by the enormity of what he was building at NASA. She wanted to understand—she did understand—but today, the waiting felt different. He had asked her to meet him here, at this park where they had spent so many afternoons when they were younger, where they had carved out quiet moments between school and home and work.

For the past year, she had been waiting for him to ask.

The thought tightened in her chest. It wasn't something they talked about

—not really—but it was something they both must have known was coming. They had been together for so long, their lives wound so tightly around one another that she could no longer picture a future where his name wasn't tied to hers. And yet, every time she thought *this is it*, every time he reached for her hand or took her somewhere special or looked at her with that soft, steady expression she had come to love, the moment would pass, and the question never came.

At first, she had been patient. Walter wasn't the kind of man to rush things. He liked plans, precision, the certainty of knowing where he was headed before he took the first step. She had told herself that it didn't matter when he asked because they both knew how this would end—with them, together, always.

Didn't they?

She glanced down at her wristwatch, the second hand sweeping forward with a certainty she envied.

She had almost stayed at the conservatory today. She should be there now, bow in hand, smoothing out the tricky phrasing in Dvořák's Cello Concerto, letting the music settle into her bones the way it always did before a performance. The Houston Youth Symphony's winter concert was next week, and she had been given a solo—a moment onstage, under the lights, her cello singing through the concert hall. It was the kind of opportunity she had dreamed of since she was a little girl, and every moment away from her music felt like a gamble, like she was losing time she couldn't afford to waste.

But Walter had asked her to meet him here.

And so she had come. She would go anywhere with Walter. She would do anything for him.

Because Walter was the love of her life. And if today—if right now—was the moment he finally asked her to be his forever, she didn't want to miss it.

Another gust of wind sent leaves skittering across the pavement, tumbling in uneven spirals before settling at her feet. She stared at them, at the way they had been carried by something unseen, something inevitable, wondering if that was what love was supposed to feel like. Was it supposed to feel something like disappointment?

She had never doubted Walter before. Never doubted that he loved her, that he wanted the same life she did. But lately, with each passing month, with each date that wasn't a proposal, a new thought had started to creep in, uninvited.

What if she had imagined it all?

What if Walter wasn't pulling away because he was busy, because he was caught up in work and time was slipping away from him faster than he realized?

What if he was pulling away because, deep down, he knew something she didn't?

The thought made her stomach twist.

She shook it off, forcing her shoulders to relax, trying not to let the lateness of the hour settle into her bones. But it was getting harder.

Because if Walter loved her as much as she loved him—if he wanted this—then why wasn't he here?

Maggie looked up at the path in front of her, empty but for the fading light stretching long over the bricks.

A few years ago, she would have given anything to be here, waiting for him, knowing he would come running toward her, breathless, apologetic, reaching for her hand like he always did.

But today, as the sun sank lower and the shadows stretched farther, she couldn't help but wonder—

What if he wasn't coming at all?

Maggie drew her bow across the strings, coaxing the final note from her cello, letting it linger, stretch, and settle into the quiet of her bedroom. She should have stopped practicing an hour ago—her fingers ached, her posture had stiffened—but she hadn't been able to bring herself to put the instrument away.

Because stopping meant thinking.

And thinking meant Walter.

Her wrist trembled slightly as she raised the bow again, shifting into another passage, something slow and aching. The music curled around her like smoke, thick enough to blur the edges of her frustration, to dull the sharp sting of waiting for him, of her sitting alone in the park as the minutes dragged by and he never arrived.

She had told herself she wasn't waiting—not really. She had convinced herself that she had chosen to stay at that bench for as long as she had, watching the golden light fade, listening to the distant sounds of the city moving around her, untouched by her disappointment.

But now, here, in the stillness of her bedroom, her hands trembled with the truth of it. She had been waiting.

And Walter never came.

Her bow stilled mid-stroke as the soft creak of her bedroom door opening broke through the music.

Maggie turned just as her mother peeked inside, her hand resting lightly on the doorknob.

"Walter's here," her mother said gently, her voice careful, knowing that Maggie had come home earlier, quiet and withdrawn, offering only that Walter must have been busy.

The words landed somewhere deep in Maggie's chest, stirring up something raw, something hot, something tangled between anger and relief.

She didn't move.

For a moment, she just sat there, her bow still poised over the strings, the cello a weight in her lap, pressing her firmly into the present.

She had spent all afternoon waiting for him, and now—now—he was here?

Her mother hesitated, studying her, as if she could see the storm beneath Maggie's stillness. "Do you want to see him?"

Maggie swallowed, her fingers flexing against the bow.

She could say no. Let him stand outside in the cold, let him wonder the way she had wondered.

But the moment the thought entered her mind, she knew she wouldn't follow through.

Because even through the hurt, even through the bitter edge of embarrassment she had carried home with her, there was something else pressing just as fiercely against her ribs.

Relief.

Because after all of it—he was here.

Maggie exhaled slowly, setting her bow down with careful precision, as if her movements could disguise the war inside her. Then she rose, smoothing the fabric of her dress with steady hands, lifting her chin just slightly.

"Yes," she murmured. "I'll see him."

Her mother nodded, stepping back, leaving the door slightly ajar.

Maggie lingered for a breath longer, then followed, her footsteps quiet against the floor, the weight of everything she wasn't saying settling into her bones.

Walter was waiting.

Maggie stepped into the sitting room, her movements measured, deliberate. The air was warm, thick with the familiar scent of her mother's lilac perfume and the faint traces of dinner lingering in the air. The soft glow from the lamp by the window bathed the room in honeyed light, casting long shadows over the floral-patterned sofa, the lace-trimmed curtains, the careful arrangement of family photographs lining the mantel.

Walter rose the instant she appeared, his movements quick, urgent, his apology already forming before his lips had fully parted.

"Maggie, I—" He exhaled sharply, running a hand through his hair, leaving it tousled, undone. "God, Maggie, I can't believe I did that to you." His voice was hoarse with regret, raw with something she couldn't quite name. "I lost track of time. I swear, I didn't mean to—"

She lifted a hand, silencing him with a quiet grace that made him pause.

"Sit down, Walter," she said, her voice even, cool as glass. She gestured toward the sofa. "Let's talk."

Outwardly, she was composed, steady. But inside—inside was something else entirely.

Relief flooded through her, fierce and unrelenting, bursting past the walls she had tried to build, rushing through her like water breaking through a dam. He was here. He was sorry. He hadn't been pulling away, hadn't been distancing himself.

And yet, beneath the relief, something sharper lurked. Because he had forgotten her.

Walter hesitated for only a second before sinking back onto the sofa, his hands clasped together, knuckles white. He looked like a man desperate to explain himself, desperate to make it right.

Maggie lowered herself into the armchair across from him, folding her hands in her lap, watching him with careful, quiet eyes.

Her mother hovered in the doorway, glancing between them, then cleared her throat softly. "Would you two like some tea?"

Maggie shook her head. "No, thank you."

Walter barely glanced up. "I'm alright, Mrs. Dawson, but thank you."

Her mother hesitated for a moment longer, then, sensing this was a conversation best left uninterrupted, gave a small nod and slipped from the room, leaving them alone.

Walter exhaled, leaning forward, resting his forearms on his knees. "Maggie," he started, his voice lower now, earnest. "I swear to you, I didn't mean to stand you up. I would never do that on purpose."

She stayed silent, watching him, waiting.

He ran a hand down his face, letting out a quiet, humourless laugh. "I was at work. We were supposed to wrap up hours earlier, but it got away from me." He met her gaze, searching for understanding. "You remember me telling you about Project Mercury?"

Maggie nodded. She didn't know the ins and outs of it like Walter did, but she had listened—really listened—every time he spoke about it. She knew it was NASA's first attempt at putting an American in space.

Walter leaned back slightly, shaking his head. "We had a telemetry issue with the Mercury-Atlas 5 flight." His voice took on that restless energy it always did when he spoke about his work, his hands gesturing as he explained. "Enos—the chimp we sent up—he wasn't supposed to complete two orbits, but when he was up there, something went wrong. A malfunction in the onboard systems." He let out a breath, shaking his head. "We had to bring him down early. There were delays, and the data wasn't coming in clean. I was running calculations, double-checking figures—Maggie, I swear, I looked up, and suddenly it was seven-thirty."

He ran a hand through his hair again, frustrated, more at himself than anything else. "I should've left earlier. I should've looked at the time. I should've—" He exhaled sharply. "I should've been there."

Maggie sat perfectly still, her heart beating in steady, measured thumps against her ribs.

She understood.

Of course she did.

But that didn't mean it didn't hurt.

Maggie inhaled slowly, steadying herself before she spoke. "Walter, I understand," she said, her voice even, measured. "I know how much your work means to you. I know how important this all is—not just to you, but to the country, to history itself." She paused, searching his face, letting her words sink in. "But you have to understand something too."

Walter nodded, leaning forward slightly, bracing himself.

"I should have been practicing today," she continued. "I have an important performance coming up—one that I've worked for my whole life. My time, my dreams, they matter just as much as yours do." She held his gaze, unwavering. "I love you, and I will always support what you do. But I need you to support me too. I can't be the only one making sacrifices."

Walter's expression softened, and he nodded again, slower this time. "You're right," he admitted, his voice quiet but full of conviction. "You're absolutely right, Maggie." He exhaled, rubbing a hand over his face. "I was so caught up in work that I didn't even think about what I was asking of you. I messed up, and I hate that I made you feel like your time, your music, wasn't just as important."

His hand found hers, his thumb brushing lightly over her knuckles. "Your dedication to the cello—your talent, your passion—it's one of the many things I love about you. I would never want you to feel like it doesn't matter." He shook his head, his voice thick with shame. "I hate that I made you feel that way today."

Maggie let his words settle in, watching the way his brows pulled together, the genuine regret in his eyes. Then, after a long moment, she shifted, moving to sit beside him on the couch.

Walter hesitated, his breath catching slightly, as if afraid of pushing his luck. But then, slowly, Maggie rose from her chair and crossed the room, settling beside him on the sofa. She hesitated only for a moment before reaching for him, slipping her arms around his waist, pressing her face against his shoulder. Walter melted into her touch, holding her tight, breathing in the familiar mix of lavender and roses that had always felt like home.

"Thank you for forgiving me," he murmured into her hair.

Maggie pulled back slightly, glancing toward the doorway to make sure her mother was nowhere in sight before settling against him again. "Just don't let it happen again," she murmured.

Walter chuckled softly. "I won't."

After a moment, he pulled back, pressing a lingering kiss to her temple. "Would you like to go for a walk with me?"

Maggie smiled, nodding. "I would."

They slipped into their coats, stepping outside into the cool night air. Walter tucked Maggie's arm through his, keeping her close as they wandered down the quiet street, the rhythm of their steps falling easily into sync. The city stretched around them, the hum of distant cars, the glow of streetlamps casting golden pools onto the pavement.

They walked south, making their way toward Buffalo Bayou Park, where the skyline flickered over the water, reflections shimmering in the gentle current. The park was quiet this late, just the occasional rustle of wind through the trees, and the distant murmur of voices from couples strolling along the pathways. The air smelled of earth and the faintest trace of winter—woodsmoke drifting from homes in the distance, mingling with the briny scent of the bayou.

Maggie sighed, resting her head briefly against Walter's shoulder as they walked. "I love this view," she murmured, watching the city lights dance over the water.

Walter stopped then, turning to face her, taking both of her hands in his.

"I love you," he said, his voice full of quiet certainty.

Maggie smiled up at him, warmth spreading through her chest. "I know," she teased gently, echoing his own words from all those times before.

Walter laughed under his breath, shaking his head. "You have no idea how much, Maggie." He lifted a hand, brushing a strand of hair from her cheek. "I love you more than I have words for. More than I know how to say. I love you when you're focused, when you're lost in your music, when you don't even see me standing there watching you in awe. I love you when you're mad at me, when you put me in my place, when you remind me of the things that matter." His voice dropped lower, reverent. "I love you so much it terrifies me."

Maggie's breath hitched, her heart hammering inside her chest.

Walter let go of one of her hands, reaching into the pocket of his wool coat.

"I meant to do this earlier," he admitted, his voice rough with emotion. "I had the whole thing planned. I was going to take you out, make it perfect. And then I messed it all up." He shook his head, a small, self-deprecating laugh escaping him. "But you—you didn't let me ruin it. You forgave me. And that's just one of the million reasons I never want to let you go."

He pulled a small velvet box from his pocket, turning it over in his fingers for a moment before sinking to one knee.

Maggie let out a soft, stunned breath, her hands flying to her mouth.

Walter opened the box, revealing a delicate gold ring, a single diamond catching the city lights. He looked up at her, his expression open, vulnerable, full of everything endless.

"Maggie Dawson," he said, his voice steady, sure. "Will you marry me?"

Maggie let out a breathless laugh, her eyes damp with unshed tears.

"Yes," she managed to breathe.

Walter let out a soft exhale, as if he had been holding his breath in for years. He rose to his feet, sliding the ring onto her finger, his hands shaking just slightly. The delicate gold band settled just above the promise ring he had given her years earlier, the two rings glinting together in the city lights—one a vow made in youth, the other a promise of forever.

Maggie stared at it, then at him, then at the city stretching wide behind them, the place where their past, present, and future had all converged into this single, perfect moment.

Then she threw her arms around him, and he caught her, holding her tight, his lips finding hers in a kiss that tasted like promise, like home.

The bayou murmured beside them, the skyline glowed above them, and the world carried on around them.

But for Walter and Maggie, time had finally stood still.

Wasn't It Beautiful
1962

Maggie set the casserole dish down on the Formica countertop, adjusting the folded kitchen towel beneath it. The scent of roasted chicken, buttered corn, and warm bread filled the small apartment, mingling with the faint hint of the bayou air that crept in through the slightly open window. She had cooked enough for two, as she always did, plating Walter's dinner beside hers before she slid into her seat at the small table.

And then she waited.

The clock on the wall ticked steadily, a rhythmic reminder of the time slipping past her. Seven o'clock came and went. Then seven-thirty. Then eight.

She picked up her fork, then set it down again. She smoothed the wrinkles in the tablecloth. She listened to the faint hum of a neighbour's radio drifting through the thin walls.

At eight-thirty, she gave up.

Her dinner had gone cold, congealing on the plate. She wrapped Walter's portion, placing it in the fridge, then rinsed off her own plate in the deep porcelain sink.

The silence of the apartment pressed in around her.

She walked into their bedroom, undressing slowly, folding her dress neatly over the chair in the corner before slipping into her nightgown. Walter's side of the bed was untouched as she slid beneath the sheets, the absence of his warmth making the cool night air feel sharper.

She stared at the ceiling, her fingers grazing the engagement ring on her left hand. They hadn't even set a date.

Every time she brought it up, Walter had some reason to wait. First, it had been his final months at Rice, then his transition to NASA, then Project Mercury. There was always something more important.

And now, she wondered if he would ever choose her at all.

Her mother's voice drifted through her thoughts, uninvited but persistent.

"You gave him everything already, Maggie. Why would he marry you when he already has the life of a married man?"

Maggie had dismissed it before, brushing it off as old-fashioned, as outdated thinking. But tonight, as she turned onto her side, pulling the blankets tight around herself, she wondered if there was truth in it.

When she woke the next morning, her face was stiff and puffy from crying, her eyes sore with the weight of sleep that had offered no rest. She turned toward Walter's side of the bed, the covers still neatly tucked, untouched.

Her stomach twisted.

He hadn't come home at all.

She got up slowly, moving through the quiet apartment, half-expecting to see him at the kitchen table, drinking coffee, apologizing for working too late.

But the apartment was still, and Walter was nowhere to be found.

The hours stretched ahead of her, long and uninviting.

By mid-afternoon, she had one thing to look forward to—her lesson. Teaching wasn't what she wanted for herself, but at least when she was working with a student, she wasn't waiting.

At exactly two o'clock, she straightened her posture and greeted her young student at the door, pasting on a warm smile that didn't quite reach her eyes. For an hour, she focused on bowing technique, phrasing, the subtle nuances of emotion that lived between the notes.

And then, just as the lesson was ending, she heard the front door open.

Walter.

He was in a hurry, moving through the apartment like a man with no time to spare. By the time Maggie bid farewell to her student and turned toward him, he was already halfway through changing his clothes, his clean work shirt buttoned hastily over a fresh undershirt.

"I have to get back," he said quickly, running a hand through his disheveled hair.

Maggie stepped forward, blocking his path before he could slip past her. "Walter."

He froze, glancing at her, then down at the engagement ring on her finger.

"You didn't come home last night," she said, her voice level, controlled. "I waited for you. I made dinner."

A flicker of guilt crossed his face, but he shook his head. "Maggie, I—"

"Sit down," she interrupted.

Walter hesitated, then let out a sigh, finally lowering himself into one of the kitchen chairs.

Maggie sat across from him, the small table between them, the remnants of last night's dinner still in the fridge, untouched.

The kitchen was modest but clean, the pale yellow cabinets chipped at the edges, a small radio sitting atop the counter, the lace curtains barely filtering the afternoon light. A chrome-edged table with matching vinyl chairs sat in the middle of the space, the kind that had been in every household like this since the early fifties. It was a space meant to be shared.

Lately, Maggie had spent too much time in it alone.

Walter ran a hand down his face, then sighed. "I'm sorry. I didn't think—"

"No, you didn't," Maggie said, her tone sharper than she intended. She exhaled, steadied herself. "Walter, I know you're busy. I know your work is important. But I can't keep coming second to it. It feels like I don't matter to you."

Walter's head snapped up. "That's not true."

"Then why won't you even set a date?" Maggie's voice had a pleading edge to it.

Walter let out a breath, his hands rubbing against his temples. "Maggie, I love you. You know that. But I can't think about a wedding right now. I just —I can't."

Maggie swallowed past the ache in her throat. "Why?"

Walter hesitated, then leaned forward, his voice low, urgent. "Because I'm working on something that matters. Do you understand that? We are trying to put a man in space. This isn't just about me. This is about history, about the future of mankind. I want to marry you, Maggie, I do. But I don't have time for frivolous things right now. I can't worry about dinner or—"

He stopped when Maggie turned her face away.

His frustration softened instantly, replaced by something like regret. "Maggie..."

Her shoulders trembled, but she didn't make a sound.

Walter reached for her hand. "I'll do better," he murmured. "I promise. But I have to go back now. I won't be home for dinner, so... don't wait up." He hesitated, then squeezed her fingers. "I'll be home to sleep. I promise."

Then he was gone.

Maggie sat there for a long time, staring at the place where he had been, at the chair still slightly pushed back from the table.

That night, she ate dinner alone.

She took a long, hot bath, steam curling around her in soft ribbons, but when she stepped out and checked the clock, it was only 8:30.

She curled up in the living room, a novel in her lap—*Ship of Fools* by Katherine Anne Porter, a book that had gripped her from the first page.

She read until her eyes blurred, the words running together, until she realized it was nearly midnight.

Walter still wasn't home.

Her heart ached as she turned off the lamp and walked into the bedroom, peeling back the blankets and slipping beneath them alone.

She buried her face in her pillow, and for the second night in a row, she cried herself to sleep.

When she woke the next morning, her face was puffy, her eyes sore.

She turned to Walter's side of the bed.

Still untouched.

Still empty.

Instinctively, she reached out.

Her fingers brushed over cold sheets.

She blinked, turning her head, her gaze settling on the untouched pillow beside her.

There was a time when this discovery would have crushed her. A time when her heart would have clenched, when her throat would have burned with unshed tears, when she would have curled into herself and willed the ache away.

But today, there was none of that.

No sharp pang of hurt. No wave of disappointment.

Just a dull, quiet acceptance.

She exhaled, long and slow, staring up at the ceiling.

She was getting used to this.

That was the worst part, wasn't it? Not the waiting, not the excuses, not the way Walter always had something more important to do.

It was that she no longer expected anything else.

She didn't wonder if he'd walk through the door. She didn't lie awake hoping to hear the familiar sound of his key turning in the lock. She just knew.

Knew he wouldn't come. Knew he wouldn't be beside her when she woke up. Knew, deep down, that she was alone, even when she wasn't supposed to be.

She turned onto her side, curling into herself, not sad, not angry—just tired, down to her very bones.

And for the first time, the thought came not as a fear, but as a quiet, unbearable truth—

This—the waiting, the loneliness, the empty space beside her—was already her life.

Maggie barely heard the sound of Walter's key turning in the lock.

She was too focused on her student, a young girl named Annie Parker, who sat on the small stool beside her, her cello tucked against her shoulder, her bow hovering over the strings. The apartment, once simply a space for her and Walter, had become something more—a place where music lived, where young students walked in with uncertainty and left with the first sparks of confidence.

She adjusted Annie's wrist with a light touch, nodding in encouragement. "Try that again, but don't rush this time. Let the notes breathe."

The apartment door swung open, and for the first time in weeks, Walter walked in not weighed down by exhaustion but practically buzzing with energy.

Maggie didn't look up right away. She had stopped expecting him at any particular hour. She certainly hadn't expected him home early.

But when she did glance toward the door, she saw him standing there, blinking, confused.

His gaze swept across the apartment, landing on the metronome ticking steadily on the coffee table, the neatly arranged music books, the small row of coats by the door—not just hers and his, but those belonging to her students.

Maggie turned back to Annie, giving no acknowledgment to Walter.

"Again," she said simply, guiding the girl through a slow, measured passage.

Walter took a step forward, still staring at the scene before him, then opened his mouth as if to speak—but stopped himself.

Maggie didn't miss the way his fingers twitched slightly at his sides. He hadn't known. Hadn't even realized how much her work had grown, how her days had filled with lessons, with students, with something that had nothing to do with him.

For the first time in a long time, he was the one left out.

Maggie felt the familiar flicker of frustration rise in her chest, but she swallowed it down, keeping her expression neutral.

She finished the lesson, dismissing Annie early with a warm smile, her tone calm even as something sharp settled inside her.

As soon as the door closed behind her student, she turned, ready to unleash every unspoken resentment, to finally say all the things she had been holding back—

But then she saw it.

Walter was grinning.

The exhaustion that had clung to him for months was gone, replaced by something bright, electric, undeniable.

"I have to tell you something," he said breathlessly.

Maggie folded her arms. "You didn't come home last night."

"I know," he said quickly, running a hand through his hair. "I—I lost track of time. But Maggie—" He stepped toward her, his entire body alive with excitement. "We did it."

She frowned, still holding on to her anger, but barely. "Did what?"

Walter let out a sharp, disbelieving laugh, like he couldn't believe the words even as he spoke them. "We cracked it. The reentry sequencing issues—we finally got it right." His words tumbled over each other, his excitement an unstoppable force. "We've been working on the heat shield stability for *Faith 7*, making sure Cooper's flight won't fail like the earlier Mercury tests. The numbers weren't aligning, and it was driving us insane. But last night, we fixed it. We have the data to prove it. *Faith 7* is ready."

Maggie blinked.

She should be angry.

She was angry.

But she also knew what this meant to him. She knew how much of himself he had poured into this, into Mercury, into NASA, into space. Silently, she resented NASA and Project Mercury for how much Walter's work meant to him.

She saw him in this moment—the boy she had fallen in love with, the boy who had always dreamed of things bigger than himself.

And despite everything—despite the lonely nights, the unanswered questions, the waiting—she smiled.

Walter let out a breathless laugh, his eyes searching hers. "Do you know what this means, Maggie? We're going to finish Mercury this year. And then —then we move forward. Gemini, Apollo, everything we've been working toward. We're one step closer."

Maggie reached for him then, a brief, instinctual touch, her hand resting lightly on his arm. "I'm proud of you, Walter," she said, and she meant it.

Walter smiled, something softer now—something settled.

And then, without warning, he took a breath, his fingers tightening slightly over hers. "I think we should set a date."

Maggie's heart stilled.

"What?" It felt like forever since Walter had proposed. Maggie, without realizing it, had begin to believe Walter would never want to set a date for their wedding.

"For the wedding." He exhaled, nodding, as if making the decision in real time. "Next year. After Mercury is done. Let's do it in March! That'll give James plenty of time to plan leave, and maybe we can even arrange to bring my mom."

Maggie's vision blurred for a second, her pulse roaring in her ears.

After all this time. After waiting and waiting. After wondering if he ever really would.

She nodded—quick, eager—before throwing her arms around him, holding on as relief crashed through her.

She had been right to wait.

She had been right to be patient.

Walter chuckled, pulling back just enough to press a kiss to her forehead.

Maggie smiled, giddy, breathless, whole. "I'm going to make you something special for dinner," she announced, already stepping toward the kitchen. "A proper celebration. Will you go get us a nice bottle of champagne?"

Walter hesitated.

It was brief, barely noticeable, but Maggie saw it.

And then he sighed, pressing a quick kiss to her temple. "I can't."

Maggie stilled.

Walter stepped away, reaching for his coat. "The team is going out for beers to celebrate."

The words sliced through her.

"Oh." It was all she managed.

Walter, oblivious, shrugged on his coat. "I won't be too late," he promised.

He smiled, squeezing her hand before stepping toward the door.

And then he was gone.

Maggie stood there, the moment she had dreamed of fading before it had even settled.

For one second—just one—she had believed tonight would be theirs. That this moment, this milestone, belonged to them.

But it never had, had it?

Because everything, always, belonged to NASA first.

She exhaled, long and slow, blinking back the sting behind her eyes.

She had waited for him before.

She would wait for him again.

She only prayed she wasn't waiting for something that would never really come.

Maggie stood frozen in the middle of their small apartment, staring at the door that Walter had just disappeared through. The echo of his voice, of his laughter, still lingered in the space around her, but he was gone.

Again.

The weight of it settled in slowly, creeping in like cold air through an open window.

She had imagined this moment so many times—the two of them celebrating together, raising glasses in their tiny kitchen, laughing, dreaming, making promises about their future. A night filled with warmth and love, something to remind her why she had waited, why she had held on, why she had convinced herself that one day, one day, he would choose her just as fiercely as he chose his work.

But she had been wrong.

Again.

Her hands trembled as she turned back toward the kitchen. She moved automatically, reaching for the cutting board, for the knife, for the vegetables she had planned to chop for dinner. She wasn't hungry anymore, but she couldn't just stand there, couldn't let herself crumble beneath the weight of another night alone, another promise half-kept, another moment stolen away by something bigger than her.

She set the knife down, gripping the edge of the counter, sucking in a sharp breath.

It wasn't anger that filled her—it wasn't even heartbreak, not exactly.

It was resignation.

A slow, creeping realization that this was their life.

That this would always be their life. With Walter, this would always be their life.

She moved numbly through the rest of the evening, skipping dinner, skipping the celebration that never came. She let the silence stretch, let it press down on her as she took a long, scalding bath, letting the water swallow her whole, as if it could drown the dull ache in her chest.

When she stepped out, the clock on the nightstand read 8:45.

She stared at it for a long time.

The hours blurred together as she curled up in the living room, picking up The Bell Jar by Silvia Plath, from where she had left it the night before. She forced herself into the story, clinging to the words like they could hold her together.

But even as the hours passed, as the apartment grew darker, she listened.

Listened for the sound of the door unlocking.

Listened for him.

9:45.

10:30.

11:15.

By 11:30, she knew.

She knew before she even stood, before she turned off the light and walked into their bedroom.

She knew before she peeled back the blankets, before she settled into the cool, empty bed.

She knew, because she had been here before.

Because she had done this so many times before.

Because she had waited before.

But tonight—tonight, she didn't cry.

She just lay there, staring at the ceiling, letting the silence fill the space where Walter should have been.

And when she woke the next morning, her body stiff, her head heavy, she already knew what she would find before she even reached across the mattress.

Walter's side of the bed was untouched.

Still cold.

Still empty.

Still waiting.

Just like her.

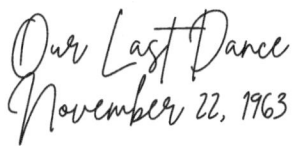

Our Last Dance
November 22, 1963

The NASA Employee Hall was alive with conversation, the hum of voices carrying through the large room. It smelled of barbecue and warm bread, the kind of comforting scent that settled into the air and made everything feel familiar, easy. Engineers, their wives, and office staff milled about, balancing plates of food, sipping from glasses of sweet tea and cold beer.

Maggie stood among a group of NASA wives, a cold glass of lemonade in her hands, listening as they swapped stories about their husbands—their long nights, their sleepless minds, the way they could be sitting at the dinner table but miles away in thought.

"And I swear," one of the women said, exasperated but affectionate, "he was about to kiss me goodnight and then stopped mid-motion to mutter something about fuel combustion efficiency."

The women laughed, a shared understanding passing between them.

Maggie smiled. For the first time in a long while, she didn't feel alone. She felt heard. She felt understood.

Walter was nearby, deep in conversation with a few of his colleagues, but every so often, his gaze flickered to her, a small smile pulling at the corner of his lips. She felt it—felt him seeing her, felt the warmth of something precious and beautiful pass between them.

It had been a perfect twenty-four hours.

The night before, they had attended a testimonial dinner at the Houston Coliseum in honour of Congressman Albert Thomas, a staunch supporter of the space program. It had been an elegant affair, with President Kennedy himself in attendance, his presence electrifying the room. Walter had been personally invited, a reflection of Thomas' deep investment in NASA's future. For one night, Maggie had been swept into Walter's world— the glow of chandeliers overhead, the hum of political conversation, the whispered nods to NASA's growing importance.

She had stood beside Walter, his hand resting lightly at her waist, as they had listened to the President of the United States reaffirm his belief in space exploration, in NASA, in the dream Walter had dedicated himself to.

For the first time in months, she had felt proud, not just of Walter, but of the life they were building together.

Now, at the celebration for NASA employees and their families, she felt that same warmth curling inside her, spreading through her limbs, making everything feel light and possible again.

A voice crackled over the loudspeaker.

"Alright, ladies and gentlemen, time for the dance contest! Last couple standing wins!"

Laughter rippled through the crowd, and Maggie turned toward Walter just as he strode toward her, a teasing smile on his lips.

"Dance with me," he murmured, offering his hand.

Maggie raised an eyebrow, smirking. "You hate dancing."

"I hate dancing," he admitted, a teasing smile tugging at his lips. "But I love dancing with you."

She laughed, allowing him to pull her toward the dance floor—a small clearing where couples were already gathering, murmuring, adjusting their grips.

The music began, a slow, swaying melody that seemed to reach inside Walter and pull something loose—something weightless, something warm.

He gathered Maggie in his arms, holding her close, feeling the press of her against him as if she had never belonged anywhere else. His touch was steady, instinctual, his palm resting at the small of her back, guiding her in time with the rhythm that neither of them had to think about.

And just like that, the rest of the world faded.

It was just them. Only ever them.

They moved together, not apart, not in passing, but as one, the way they always had when nothing else was pulling him away. When there were no unfinished calculations waiting for him, no moon to reach for, no world outside of her.

Maggie tipped her head back, her laughter slipping into the space between them like a quiet melody all its own. "Alright, I'll admit it. You're better than I remember."

Walter smiled, his grip tightening slightly, holding them steady in the moment. He spun her gently, watching as the hem of her dress lifted with the movement, catching the air like the soft sweep of a brushstroke on canvas.

"I could say the same about you," he murmured.

It was effortless.

Like they had been dancing forever. Like they had never stopped.

He took in everything—the way her hair brushed against her shoulders, the way her perfume mixed with the warm air, the way she fit against him, as if she had been made to.

For once, he wasn't thinking about anything else. Not about NASA, not about calculations, not about where he had to be next.

He was here.

He was hers.

Maggie closed her eyes, resting her head lightly against his shoulder, and Walter felt something in him settle, something that had been restless for too long.

This was them.

This was everything.

He dipped his head, his lips brushing against her ear, his voice quiet but certain. "I love you, Maggie."

She smiled against him, her arms tightening around his neck. "I love you, too."

Walter exhaled softly, pressing a kiss to her temple, slow and reverent, like a promise. He lingered there for a moment, his breath warm against her skin, his hold on her unwavering. Then, in a voice just for her, low and certain, he whispered, "I can't wait to marry you in March."

Maggie closed her eyes, letting the words settle inside her, wrapping around her like the warmth of his embrace. She could feel the truth of it in the way he held her, in the way his lips brushed against her hair, in the steady rhythm of his heartbeat against hers.

For the first time in so long, she let herself believe—really believe—that nothing could take this away from them.

And then—

A crackle over the loudspeaker.

The music cut off.

A voice—shaky, uncertain—broke through the static.

"Ladies and gentlemen, we have an important announcement..."

The world stilled.

"...President John F. Kennedy has been shot in Dallas."

For a moment, no one moved.

The couples on the dance floor stood frozen in place, their hands still clasped, their bodies still poised as if waiting for the next beat to drop. A murmur swept through the room—quiet at first, then growing, voices overlapping in confusion, disbelief.

Maggie's breath hitched as she turned her gaze up to Walter, her fingers tightening in his. He wasn't moving either. His eyes had darkened, his jaw set, his entire body rigid.

The words didn't make sense.

Kennedy had been here. Last night. Right here in Houston. She had seen him, had watched him smile, had listened to him speak with the kind of conviction that made her believe in everything Walter had dedicated himself to.

And now he had been shot.

Someone near the back of the room whispered, "No, no, no," over and over again, the words barely more than breath. A woman let out a soft, stunned gasp. A man removed his hat, clutching it to his chest.

Maggie still wasn't moving.

She felt Walter's hand tighten at her waist, keeping her steady, keeping her there, but she wasn't sure she was really standing anymore. The floor felt unsteady beneath her feet, like the world had shifted, like the very foundation of everything had cracked without warning.

Across the room, a radio had been switched on, the hum of static filling the hall. Voices hushed, strained toward it, waiting, clinging to every word like the right one might make this moment untrue.

And then—

Walter Cronkite's voice came through, steady but heavy with something deep, something irrevocable.

"From Dallas, Texas... the flash, apparently official... President Kennedy died at 1 p.m. Central Standard Time."

A strangled noise escaped Maggie's throat.

Tears blurred her vision before she could stop them, hot and immediate, spilling onto her cheeks as she pressed her hands to her mouth.

Walter turned to her instantly, his hands coming up to hold her face, brushing away the tears with his thumbs even as his own eyes shone with something restrained, something held back only by sheer force of will.

"Oh, Maggie," he murmured, voice breaking. He pulled her into his chest, pressing his lips to her hair, holding her like he could shield her from it, like he could make this moment anything but what it was.

All around them, the room had collapsed into grief. Women were crying, men stood silent and stunned, shaking their heads as if the motion alone could undo what had just been said. Some whispered prayers, others just stood there, lost, unmoored in the weight of it.

Then, a figure emerged from the crowd, stepping toward Walter.

James E. Webb, the administrator of NASA.

Maggie had met him once, briefly, at a formal function months ago. A commanding presence, a man who carried the weight of the space program on his shoulders. Now, his face was grave, his expression unreadable as he reached Walter, lowering his voice just enough that Maggie had to strain to hear.

"Walter, I need you," Webb said, his tone clipped but urgent. "Emergency meeting. The vice president is in the air, about to be sworn in. We don't know what this means for us yet."

Walter pulled back from Maggie, glancing between her and Webb, something unreadable flashing across his face before he gave a sharp nod.

Maggie already knew what was coming before he turned to her.

"I have to go," he said, his voice low, regretful. He brushed his hands down her arms, trying to steady her, but she was already breaking apart.

"Walter..." Her voice was pleading.

One of the other NASA wives, Evelyn Conrad, stepped forward, her eyes red-rimmed but full of understanding. "Maggie, I'll drive you home."

Walter exhaled, relieved, grateful. He cupped Maggie's face once more, pressing a lingering kiss to her forehead, then her lips, whispering against them, "I love you. I'll come home as soon as I can."

And then he was gone.

Maggie stood there, lost in the middle of the room as the world around her fell apart.

The voices around her blurred into a low hum, overlapping whispers of disbelief, grief, and quiet prayers. Someone turned the radio up, but the words no longer made sense.

Maggie barely registered the movement around her—the shifting bodies, the soft sobs, the way some people pressed handkerchiefs to their faces while others simply stood there, staring at nothing.

She let her gaze fall to the empty space where Walter had been just moments ago, where his warmth had still lingered against her skin. The room felt colder without him.

Her fingers trembled at her sides. She swallowed, but the lump in her throat didn't move.

Someone touched her shoulder—Evelyn, maybe. Maggie nodded numbly, not sure what she was agreeing to.

She glanced around, as if looking for something to hold on to, some proof that the world was still intact, that it hadn't just shattered in front of them.

But all she saw were people caught in the same terrible stillness.

Nothing would ever be the same again.

She exhaled slowly, blinking against the tears that still wouldn't stop, as the weight of history settled around them, pressing down like a heavy, unshakable silence.

The Music In My Mind

2025

Walter sat in his kitchen, the dim morning light slanting through the lace curtains, casting long shadows across the worn wooden table. The air smelled of stale coffee and time—of years that had slipped through his fingers, of a life that had moved forward without him fully realizing it.

In front of him, the newspaper lay open, its ink-smudged pages untouched. His coffee had long gone cold, but he held the mug anyway.

Maggie's name was still there, printed in black and white. He had read it again this morning, just as he had every morning since he first saw it. As if, by some miracle, the words might change, as if he might flip the page and find that she was still here, still somewhere, waiting for him.

He traced the edge of the paper with his thumb. Sixty-two years. Sixty-two years since that last dance. And in all that time, he had never danced again.

Why would he?

The only person he had ever wanted to dance with was gone.

His eyes drifted to the drawer beside the sink, the one he rarely opened anymore. He knew what was inside. Knew it was waiting for him, just as it had for decades.

Slowly, he set down his coffee and reached for the handle.

The drawer groaned in protest, the wood sticking from years of disuse. Inside, buried beneath old receipts and scraps of paper, was a single folded note, its edges worn soft from the years, from the nights he had taken it out just to hold it, just to see her handwriting again.

His fingers trembled as he unfolded it.

Walter,
I can't do this anymore.

I have loved you for so long, longer than I even knew how to name it. And I thought that love could be enough. I thought if I was patient, if I waited, if I held on a little longer, that you would find a way to meet me here, in this life we were supposed to have.

But I see it now. You have always been reaching for something just beyond me, something I can never be. And I can't keep waiting for you to choose me over the stars.

I hope you reach them, Walter. I hope you do everything you set out to do. But I can't keep being the thing you leave behind.

Goodbye.
Maggie

His breath shuddered as he let the words sink in—words he had read a thousand times, words that had never stopped cutting deep into his skin and piercing his heart.

He had never responded. What was there to say? He had come home that night, found the apartment empty, the echoes of her still lingering in the walls, in the way the chair at the kitchen table was pushed back just so, as if she had hesitated before leaving.

He had thought about chasing her. Had imagined himself running to her parents' house, knocking on the door, falling to his knees, begging her to stay.

But he hadn't.

Because he had made his choice long before that moment.

He had made it every time he walked out the door, every time he let work take precedence, every time he let the silence stretch too long between them.

And Maggie—God, Maggie had loved him anyway.

But love had never been the problem.

Love had been the only thing that had ever come easy.

It was everything else that had failed them. It was Walter himself that had failed them.

Walter ran a hand over his face, exhaling sharply. The years felt heavy now, pressing down on his chest, on his ribs. He was old. He was tired. And Maggie—Maggie was gone.

He looked out the window, at the wide stretch of land beyond his kitchen, at the oaks swaying lazily in the breeze.

He closed his eyes.

And he could see her.

Not as she had been in those last days, when the fights had worn them down, when the love between them had been tangled up in waiting and regret.

But as she had been that afternoon in 1963, beneath the soft glow of the NASA hall.

Her hair catching the light, her blue eyes bright with laughter. The warmth of her body pressed against his, the music carrying them through the steps of a dance that had felt endless.

She had been looking at him like he was the only thing that mattered.

And he had believed, for a moment, that he could be.

That he could love her the way she needed, the way she deserved.

But love had never been the problem.

His fingers tightened around the letter.

Walter stood, moving to the record player in the corner of the room, the one he hadn't touched in years.

He ran his hands over the familiar grooves, the dust-coated edges of an old vinyl he had nearly forgotten.

He set the needle down.

The first notes of a song crackled to life, soft and slow.

Walter closed his eyes.

And, for the first time in sixty-two years, he let himself dance.

The kitchen faded away.

The years melted.

And in his mind, Maggie was there, laughing, twirling, looking at him like he had never let her go.

The music swelled, carrying them back, back to that day, back to that last dance.

He swayed, whispering the words under his breath.

Walter closed his eyes, the room shifting around him, the years folding in on themselves. The weight of time thinned, stretched, unraveled.

And then—

There she was.

He could feel her. The warmth of her hand in his, the soft press of her fingertips along his palm, the ghost of her breath against his cheek.

The music swelled, filling the empty kitchen, filling the quiet that had lived inside him for so long.

Walter moved, his steps slow, measured, and for the first time in years, he wasn't dancing alone.

Maggie was here.

He didn't know if she had come to him, or if he had finally found his way back to her.

But it didn't matter.

They moved together, just like they had that afternoon, just like they had in a hundred other imagined moments, just like they had always meant to.

He could hear her laughter, light and unburdened, feel the way her dress brushed against his legs as he spun her. She was radiant, weightless, young and golden.

Walter exhaled, his voice breaking as he whispered, "It was good, wasn't it?"

Maggie tilted her head up at him, smiling in that way she used to, the way that made the whole world feel bright and endless.

"It was everything," she whispered back.

His throat tightened.

He pulled her close, held on like he could make this last, like he could keep her here, keep the years from stealing her away again.

But she was already slipping, already fading, already turning to light in his arms.

Walter's breath hitched, but he didn't stop.

He danced.

Because she was still here.

Because she was still his Maggie.

And he was still hers.

Even if he had let her go.

Even if it was too late.

Even if all they had left was this—

A single, fleeting moment.

A moment that had once been everything.

You've reached The End But...
The Stories Never Stop

Songs To Stories is exactly what is sounds like - short, emotionally devastating, romantically charged, and occasionally unhinged novellas inspired by the one and only Taylor Swift. Because why simply listen to a song when you can spiral into an entire fictional universe about it?

A new novella drops the 13th of every month, so if you have commitment issues, don't worry - you don't have to wait long for your next dose of heartbreak, longing, and characters making wildly questionable life voices in the name of love.

To keep up with the latest releases, visit BrittWolfe.com - or don't, and risk missing out while the rest of us are already crying over the next one. Your call.

See you at the next emotional wreckage.

About The Author

Britt Wolfe

Britt Wolfe was born in Fort McMurray, Alberta, and now lives in Calgary, where she battles snow, writes stories, and cries over Taylor Swift lyrics like the proud elder Swiftie she is. She loves being part of a fan base that's as passionate as it is melodramatic.

She's married to a smoking hot Australian (her words, but also probably everyone else's), and together they parent two fur-babies: Sophie, the most perfect husky in the universe, and Lena, a mischievous cat who keeps them on their toes—and their furniture in shreds.

When Britt's not writing or re-listening to "All Too Well (10 Minute Version)," she's indulging her love for reading, potatoes in all forms, and the colour green. She's also a huge fan of polar bears, tigers, red pandas, otters, Nile crocodiles, and—because they're underrated—donkeys.

Her life is full of love, laughter, and just enough chaos to keep things interesting.

 @the.banality.of.britt

 BrittWolfe.com